I NY
W9-DDP-827

D.JUDE.MILLER
publishing

presents

Read the book, then solve the riddle.
Find the hidden word on each monster page and connect the sentence.

Monsters
in
MANHATTAN
2

QUEENS, NY
FIRST DAY OF
SUMMER VACATION

The breeze nudged me awake, the sun ready to bake.
After nine grueling months, I was due for a break.
Sayonara, homework. Adios, Mrs. McFlynn.
You can hit the road, math. Bounce on outta here, gym.
Ciao, spelling. Bye, grammar. So long, punctuation.
School's finally over. Hello, summer vacation!

No more rising at dawn now that classes are gone.
Ninety days to myself, I stretched out with a yawn.
Three whole months to unwind, all those long sunny days–
Pool parties, bike riding and some firework displays.
Barbeques at the beach and a ball game or two,
I believe I deserve it with what school puts kids through.

Sleepy-eyed, matted hair, I slid out toward the stairs,
There to see at the bottom stood my crew-cut nightmare.
Jimbo Joe was his name, Mary Lou's older brother.
Seriously, Mom?! I need to talk to my mother.
I was frozen with fear so I barely remember
When my Mom explained how he would stay 'til September!

JUNE 24TH
SUMMER!
JUNE 23RD
SUMMER!
JUNE 22ND
SUMMER!
JUNE 20th
LAST DAY
OF SCHOOL!

JUMBO
JUG

All through breakfast he stared, the whole time he just glared.
Mary Lou was annoying, Jimbo Joe had me scared.
Then when Dad left the room, his paw grabbed my throat -- Choke!!
Jimbo yanked my face closer and he finally spoke.
"I know what you did. Now I'll pound you to pulp."
I'm a dead man. I'm done. If I could swallow, I'd gulp.

Mary Lou must have squealed and my fate now was sealed.
I tried, "Sorry! Just kidding?" but his grip didn't yield.
With a mouth full of eggs, he went on to explain,
A pre-scheduled plan with three months' worth of pain.
"Upper body in June, July knees, ankles, thighs.
Then in August," he smirked, "let's keep that a surprise."

So, then came the request, "Entertain our fine guest."
My response was a laugh and a "Surely you jest?!"
I fought hard and said no, but Mom sternly insisted,
And with Jimbo, my arm was quite literally twisted.
I pleaded, I begged, even faked diarrhea
But again I was off as Manhattan sightseer.

Well, you know the routine, the same horrible scene,
Squashed in the back seat like a frightened sardine.
Dad drove and told stories enjoying the ride.
Jimbo smiled, driving elbows right into my side.
While my Mom applied sunscreen, making sure no skin's missed,
Jimbo J applied pressure to my gut with his fist.

I was totally stunned since I thought that I'd won.
I forgot that my aunt had this terrible son.
Mary Lou was horrendous, that's without much debate.
Jimbo Joe's at least double both the trouble and weight.
He smells twice as bad and he sweats like a boar.
A pear-shaped avenger here to settle the score.

With another abuser, I felt like a loser.
Was my whole summer lost to this turnip-truck bruiser?
I was left with no choice, now I must pull the trigger.
When your problems get larger, then your monsters get bigger.
By the end of the day, he will wish he was Mary.
Oh Jimbo, poor Jimbo, it's about to get scary.

THE METROPOLITAN MUSEUM OF ART

And so now we depart for the Museum of Art
With its Monets, Rembrandts and Van Goghs.
But while you critique, you just might catch a peek
Of the Gremlin that signs "Impasto."

This shape-shifting creature could be an art teacher,
Since he knows all the artists and facts.
But there's only one flaw, this smart monster can't draw
And his work is too grossly abstract.

When his paint-dripping feet run across a Magritte
He can pose in the frame as a queen.
Then no longer be crowned when your head spins around
To check out what your eyes may have seen.

He is quite the art vandal, causing all sorts of scandals
When adding his mark with a splash.
Yeah, a museum's curator turned an Impasto hater
When Mona Lisa received a mustache!

No, you never can tell, if in that Raphael,
He is plotting his next victim's fall.
So, I wouldn't get close or you'll end up like those
Who were caught and now hang on the wall.

IMPASTO
GOTHAM'S

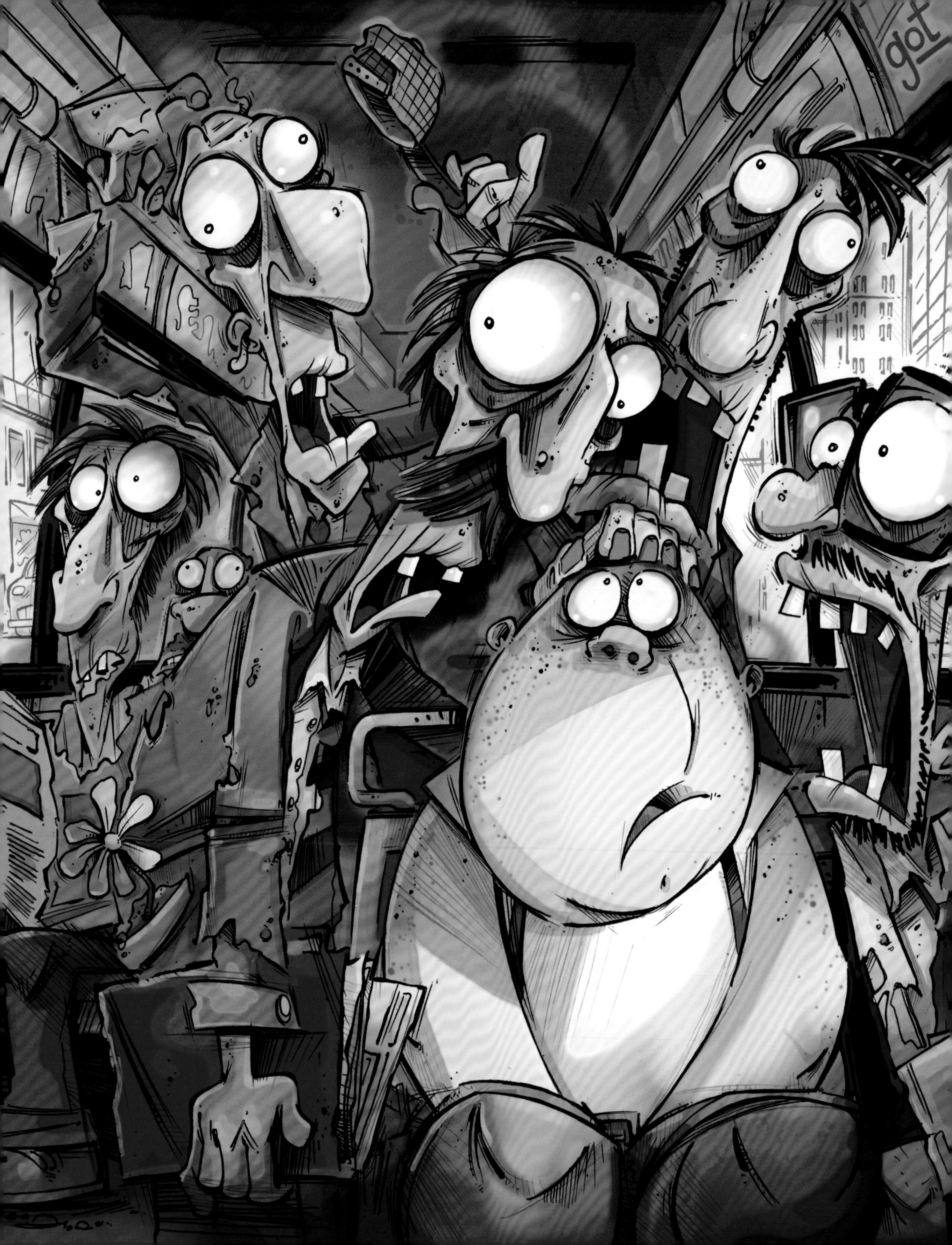
got

tHE BUS

It's Monday. It's early. It's blazingly hot.
So we'll jump on a bus to get to our next spot.
The A/C is busted so it won't help a lot,
And it smells like these riders have started to rot.

Yup, zombies, dirt-nappers, the walking undead.
They don't hunger for sweets, meat, fruit, eggs or bread,
A lone menu request that they want to be fed.
I will give you a hint: you have one in your head.

These guys are quite simple, there's not much to explain,
Once successful stock brokers sipping fine French Champagne.
Now a dome full of worms where no ideas remain.
Just one thought in their skulls: brains, brains, brains, brains,
brains, brains.
Having brains on the brain makes the lunch choice a breeze.
It's brains. Just plain brains. With no fries, hold the cheese.
You can keep your fast food. They don't care for Chinese.
It's brains, only brains, some more brains if you please.

Zombies love eating brains with no care how it's served,
On a plate, in a bucket, even straight off the curb.
A big brain on a bun can be truly superb.
Maybe Jim's tiny brain could become an hors d'oeuvre?

EVERY CORNER

It's hard finding space in this cramped concrete maze.
With a shortage of housing, there are plenty of strays.
If I told you how many, you'd be shocked and astounded.
It's just safe to assume you're completely surrounded.

See those twenty black bags in a great garbage wall?
Well, they're filled up with goblins and no garbage at all.
A mail box? For what? Who sends letters now, kid?
It's become the address for a squashed purple squid.

Plastic things with free junk I'm sure nobody wanted-
They are home to dark shadows and like, totally haunted.
Under scaffolds in place during building repair,
Look up! Starving spiders! Guess you better beware!

Each crack, every crevice, is crawling with creeps,
Like the ones from your dreams watching you while you sleep.
The hydrants hide horrors, bus shelters shield spooks,
Yet there's still only germs in abandoned phone booths.

What I'm trying to say is you're always defenseless.
Specters, pygmies and imps, the list's virtually endless.
Yeah, get used to it, bro. Sorry, have to suggest it.
There's not "some" monsters here. No, I'd say we're infested!

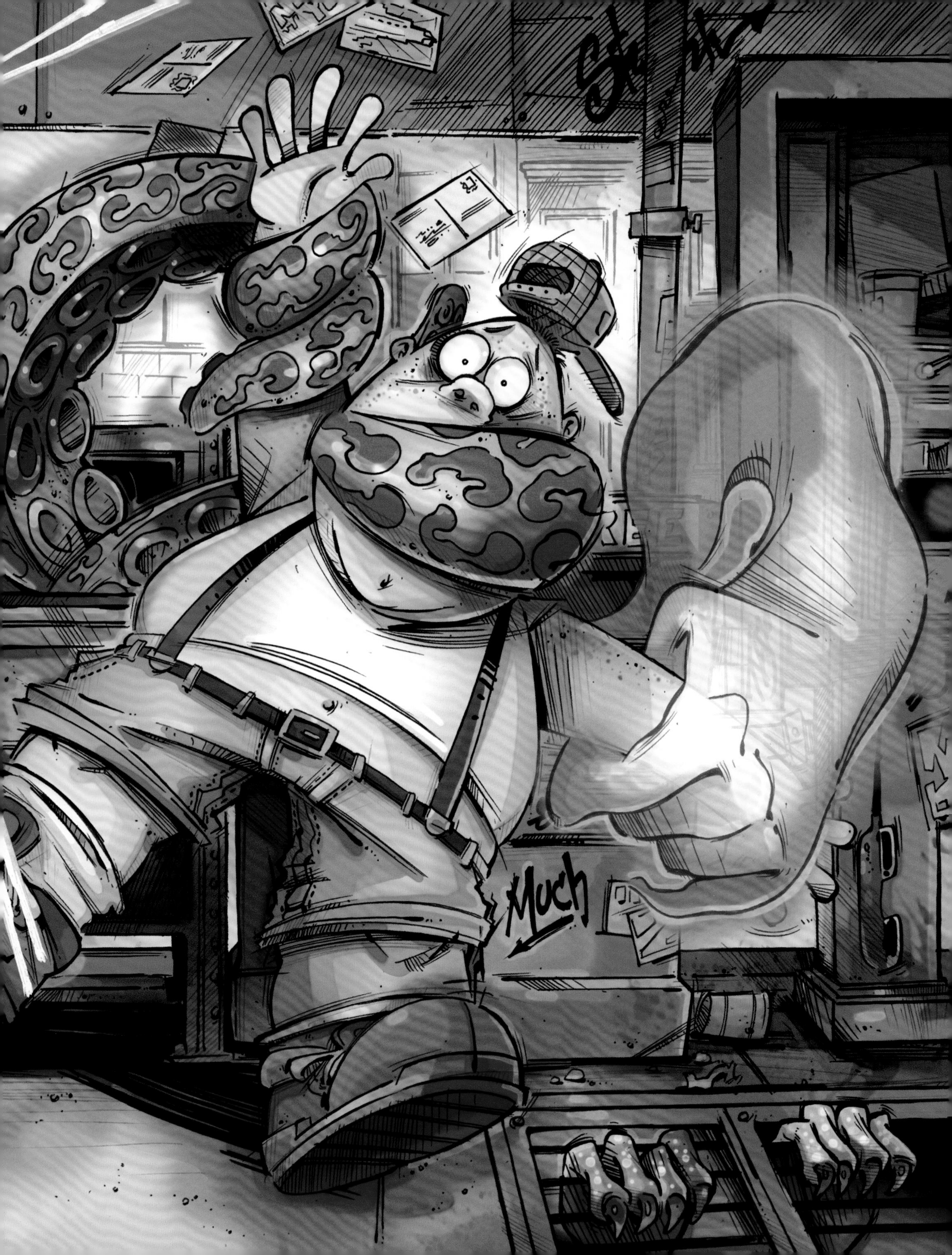
Much

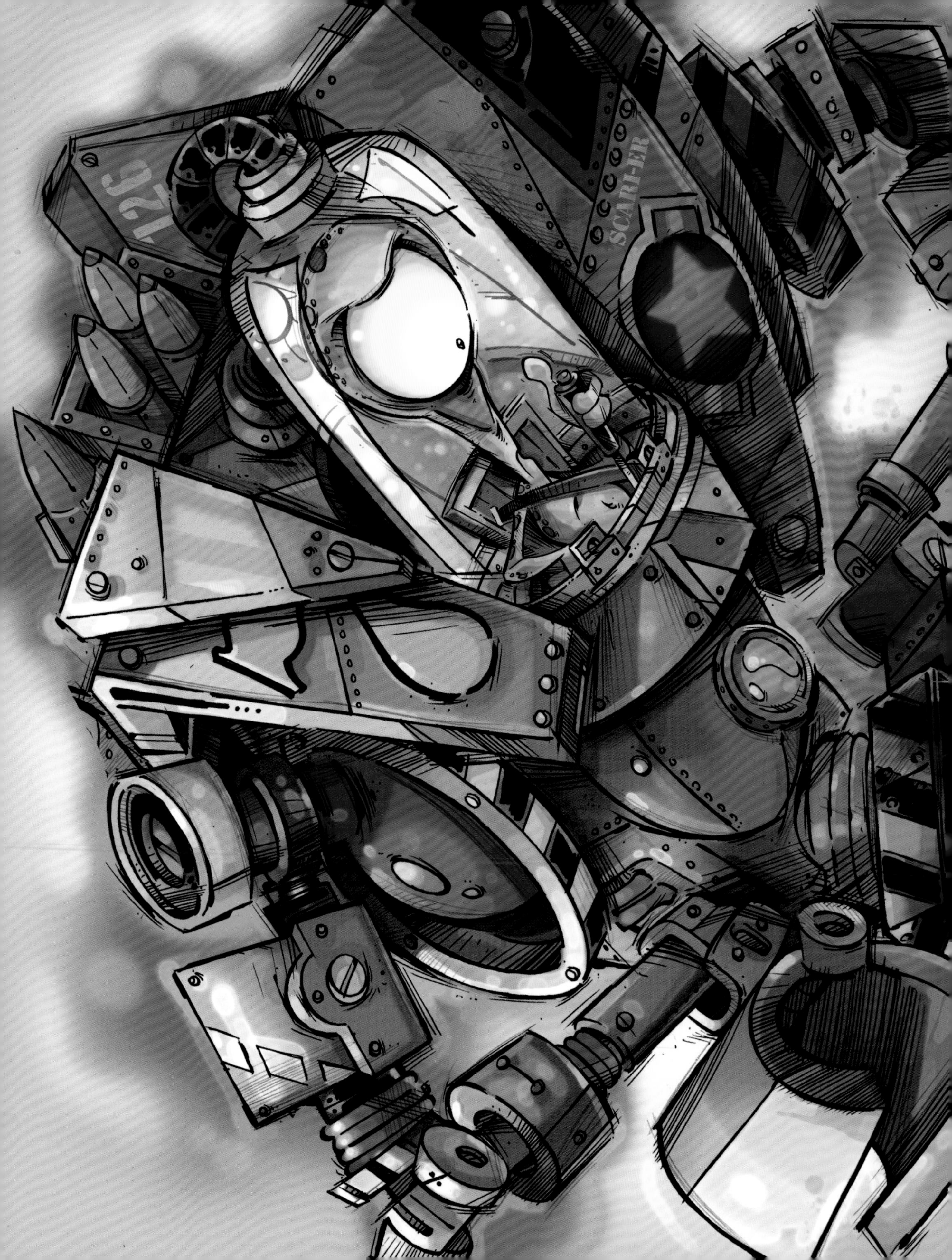
126
SCARI-ER

THE INTREPID SEA, AIR & SPACE MUSEUM

Tremble! Fall to your knees! Or you'll be crushed like fleas
By your new cosmic alien master!
At least that was the plan. He came, nobody ran.
This invasion thing's been a disaster.

His galactic attack ended totally whack.
Children laughed at his puny space drone.
Nightly news never showed and his saucer got towed
'Cause he parked in a no-standing zone.

This hopeless invader tried to zap a train later,
No one fainted or scattered or hid.
He was completely ignored, then shoved right out the door.
Some jerk yelled, "Nice costume there kid!"

Seems his intel was botched. The sci-fi films he'd watched
Showed the humans all helpless and weak.
He was certainly tricked by those black and white flicks.
Color earthlings are harder to freak.

Learn this humbling lesson; Gotta bring bigger weapons
To scare folks that are modern and jaded.
So, with stolen ship parts, armor, missiles and darts,
This runt Martian got jacked and upgraded!

the MAIn LiBRaRY

Okay, Double J, let's hit the library,
To check on our senior, gray adversary.
Morzok the warlock, the dragon's past rival,
Who misplaced his spell book upon his arrival.

The wizard and lizard scuffled, struggled and scrapped
Across six generations and all over the map.
He regrets, he forgets, how these chums became foes
But ill will can still thrive after memory goes.

Like most feuds among dudes, a young girl caused this mess.
A blonde beautiful damsel they both wished to distress.
She soon fled and was wed to a brave cavalier,
While these two former pals fought for three hundred years.

Now Zok's trapped like a sap in this Black Magic section.
Revenge is exhausting on further reflection.
Maybe "pals before gals" is the truth in the end.
He got lost in the grudge and it cost him a friend.

Look, a sage at his age becomes fragile and weak.
His good eye's gotten foggy and now both his hips creak.
Yet, while old, don't be bold and do not get me wrong,
While his legs might be shaky, his spell hand is still strong!

Things

CANDLES
$7
$6
$6
$9

the STREET FESTIVAL

Festivals, street festivals! C'mon Jimbo let's go!
The streets are blocked off. You can snag some fried dough.
All the vendors have come with their items in tow.
Like those huge lemonades and alpaca ponchos.

These nomadic merchants, no storefront to call home.
Sidewalk salesmen set free, every weekend to roam
The flea markets and fairs from Bayside to Bayonne,
Always lugging their trinkets of crystal and stone.

Are their relics from ruins? From lands rugged and rough?
Were they wrestled from rulers both wicked and tough?
Surviving an age when brute strength was enough?
Nope. They're all made in China, just like most of our stuff.

But that's not all they got, there's a bunch more to find!
Scented candles and oils heal your body and mind.
A book to gain focus if your third eye's gone blind
And an awesome massage keeps your spine all aligned.

Some say this junk works for what achy souls yearn.
That they'll heal and enlighten, or at least ease life's burn.
But if they're hoaxes instead, your receipt's pretty stern.
It reads: ALL SALES ARE FINAL! NO EXCHANGES! NO RETURNS!!

GREENWICH VILLAGE

Greenwich Village is hip, trendy, stylish and cool.
Most stand out with tongue rings and tattoos.
But that fails to compare with a marbleized stare
And a venomous hissing hairdo.

Meet Medusa from Crete, now of Christopher Street,
She left Greece ‘cause she didn’t fit in.
All the gods and the heroes made her feel like a zero,
Making fun of her scaly snake skin.

Mount Olympus was lame. All those squares were the same.
So she bolted, left them in the past.
She’d find alts, goths and punks - no more judgmental junk -
North of Houston, a real home at last.

Need some ink of a rose or a ring through your nose?
Try the body mod shop that she owns.
But pick wise, understand, it’s a permanent brand.
I’m not kidding, her work’s etched in stone.

Most tat artists confirm how much people will squirm,
They try not to, but certainly will.
Yet her clients don’t flinch from the sting or the pinch.
Everyone sits surprisingly still.

OOTTAT
PENGUINS
DAD

Hey Jimbo, you hungry? Wanna grab a quick slice?
And a big frosty cola overflowing with ice?
Just a word to the wise: Keep your neck well protected,
Since I've heard that this place could be vampire connected.

Look, way in the back, of this place that they run,
There are three soulless diners all avoiding the sun.
No reflections, black capes, with large ancient medallions,
Sharp fangs and white faces, I don't think they're Italians.

“It’s my pizza they love,” says the owner Fat Tony,
“One likes sausage, one onions and one pepperoni.
Hey! These bloodsuckers hate Transylvanian cuisine.
If you’ve tried the bat stew, then you’d see what they mean.”

Try calzones or strombolis, they’re the best that I’ve had.
And strangely enough, the blood pudding ain’t bad.
Still, this place can get mobbed without drawing a crowd.
Do ya hear what I’m sayin’? Don’t repeat that too loud.

Here a stake could be useful or some water that’s blessed
But if you want to be safe, “mind your business” is best.
If you whip out the garlic, they will tell you to shove it.
'Cause forget what ya heard. Here in New York they love it!

THE HUDSON RIVER

Why so woozy there, chum? Something wrong with your fruit?
You seasick? Or just spooked by our watery brute?
This one's got a name, and it's Kipsy - Aww cute -
The crustacean mutation formed when people pollute.

He's big fish in this pond, the king crab of this bay.
Try a dip in the drink and you're on the buffet.
Take some laps in the Hudson? You'll become a fillet.
And he'll swallow you raw, forget poached or sautéed.

He's the Beast of East River and all waters around.
A pure eating machine and the champ pound for pound,
Gobblin' guppies from here out to Long Island Sound.
Jersey Shore's got good grub since they're oiled and browned.

Wanna tussle with Kipster? Then you better not skimp.
All his foes in the past left with more than a limp.
The Kraken be lackin'. Moby Dick's a white wimp.
That Nessie is lessie. As for Jaws, he's a shrimp.

Better watch when you lean, taking in the great view.
Did you check that old rail? Notice any loose screws?
A mishap or a slip and the balance you lose
Turns this fine ferry ride into Kip's dinner cruise.

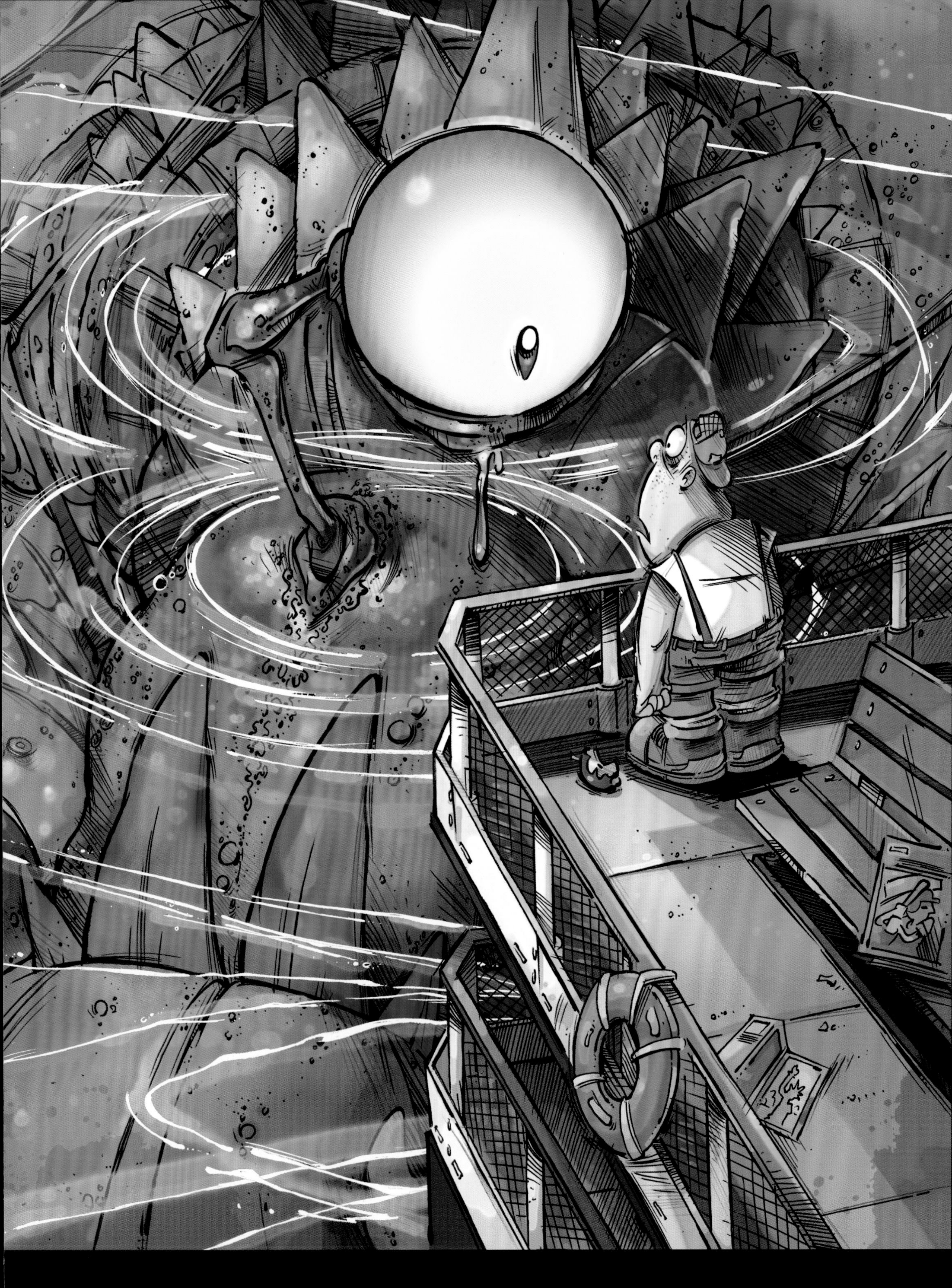

Tut and Sphinx loved high jinx – couple Cairo class clowns
Always teasing each other and fooling around.
Just two friends goofing off with, like, no inhibitions.
Trading tricks, they were locked in a prank competition.

It's too bad Sphinx got mad when a problem arose.
This one ruse went too far, into real "got your nose."
The stunts stopped, the cons closed with that cosmetic gaffe.
And yet still the Sphinx swore he would have the last laugh.

Pranks aside, the king's pride was his posh pyramid,
A triangular vault where his valuables hid.
It was built, to the hilt, a deluxe pointy number.
And the perfect resort for an eternal slumber.

When Tut croaked, came the joke. Yup, the old switcheroo.
Sphinxy planned it for years, a real comedy coup.
Tut assumed his lush tomb was his final address,
But "somehow" he got sealed in a big copper dress.

What a hoot! Substitute the East River for Nile!
But Wraps isn't amused, not a hint of a smile.
No Egypt for his crypt. Huh, I thought it was funny!
Seems like Pharaohs get gags. There's no humor in mummies.

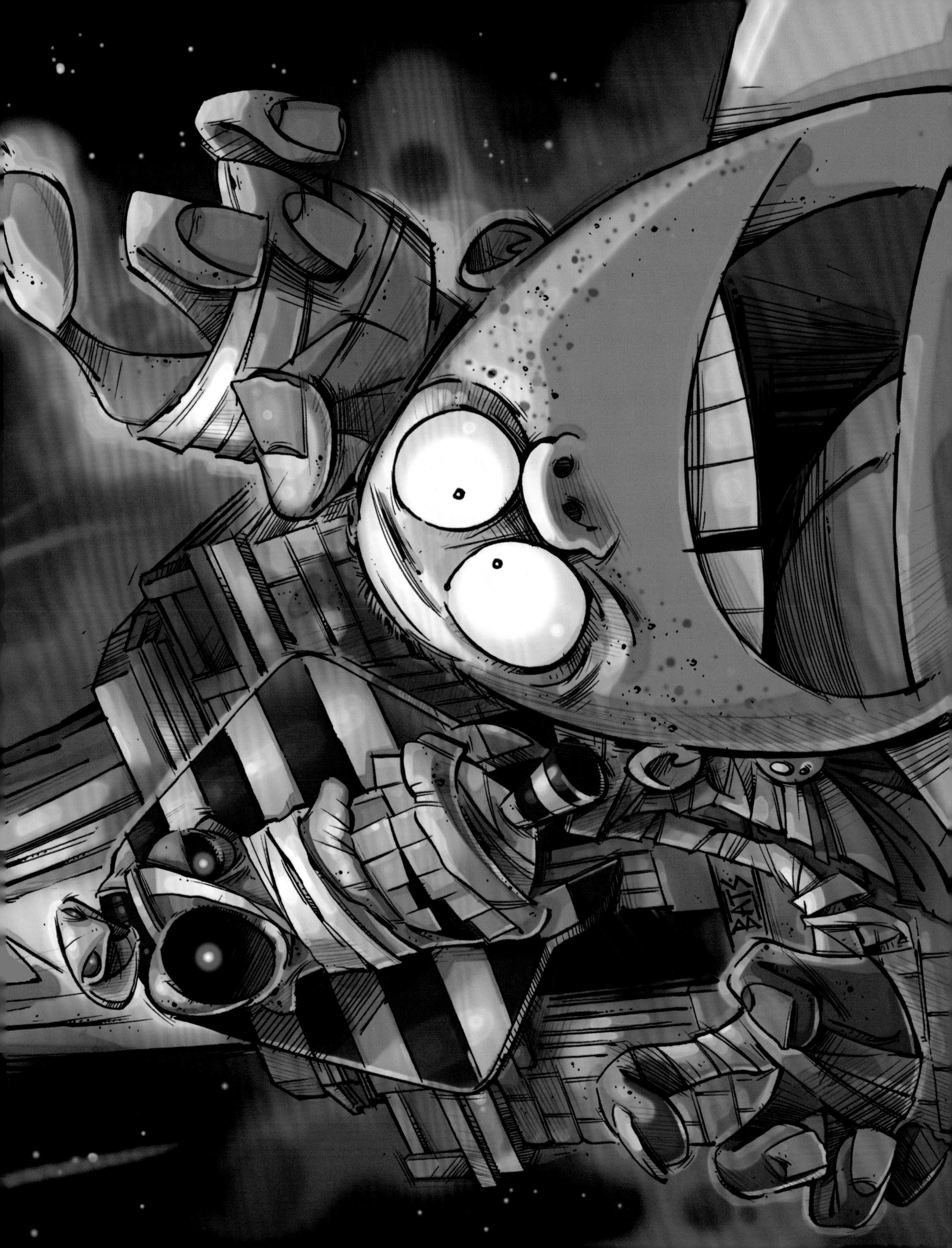

Just like that I was freed. Plans tomorrow? No need.
Jimbo stayed one last night, then checked out with light speed!
And by sunrise was gone. Off to? Well, I don't care.
Sweaty sheets the last sign that he ever was there.
Looks like he was a chump, only talked a good game.
And no match for my monsters. Yeah, it's really a shame.

After all of his threats that got me so upset,
I disposed of him quick, without breaking a sweat.
My tormentor dried up, all his anger had fizzled.
The big, bad, bald, blimp wilted, withered and shriveled.
Now, the future was bright, those dark clouds in the rear
And unlike Jimbo's face, my whole August was clear.

See ya, Joe! Buh-Bye, J! It's a shame you won't stay.
I'm just teasing. I'm psyched that you're going away!
I popped my pal Jim like a size XL blister.
Who'd've thought he'd be chicken far worse than his sister?
If you came to my home, would you act like a pest?
Is it too much to ask for a kind, welcome guest?

NY
1:29

I skipped ‘cross the floor, my vacation restored.
Make that two bullies down, if you’ve been keeping score.
This was easy, no prob. With a few well-placed beasts,
I turned Jimbo’s long summer into something more brief.
Put another fright trophy there up on my shelf.
Sometimes I’m so good, I scare even myself!

I took a big plastic cup and then filled it all up –
Doughnuts, ice cream and milk mixed together there. Yup!
You want waffles for breakfast? Well, I’d rather have fudge
Eaten out on my stoop. I’d prefer you not judge.
When I’m done with my food and my mood has been cooled
Then it’s time to suit up for a dive in the pool!

Ahhhhhh. Listen and glisten. Let the sun dry your arms.
Summer’s singing its song of birds and car alarms.
That’s Queens in July and the sounds that I treasure.
It seems endless right now, but it won’t last forever.
One last piece of advice, and I hate to remind you.
Enjoy all these days off. School will come back to find you!

SUN'S OUT.
GUNS OUT.
BUNS

LIFEGUARD
SUGAR
$1

THE EnD.

Nah, THERE'S still MORE.

Written & Illustrated
by
Daniel Jude Miller

Monsters in Manhattan 2

First printing April 2017

ISBN - 10: 0-692-87767-3
ISBN - 13: 978-0-692-87767-8

www.djudemiller.com

D.JUDE.MILLER
publishing

Printed in PRC

Daniel Jude Miller

Thank you to all of the children, parents, friends and family
who have enjoyed, supported and inspired me
through the book-making process, again.

You know what's even better than realizing your dream?
Realizing it twice!